Natalja's Stories

T0357184

Inger Christensen

Natalja's Stories

A NOVEL

*translated from the Danish
by Denise Newman*

A NEW DIRECTIONS PAPERBOOK ORIGINAL

Published by arrangement with Gyldendal Group Agency

First published as New Directions Paperbook 1633 in 2025
Manufactured in the United States of America

Library of Congress Cataloging-in-Publication Data
Names: Christensen, Inger, 1935–2009, author. |
Newman, Denise J., translator.
Title: Natalja's stories : a novel / by Inger Christensen ;
translated from the Danish by Denise Newman.
Other titles: Nataljas fortællinger. English
Description: First edition. |
New York : New Directions Publishing Corporation, 2025.
Identifiers: LCCN 2024058702 | ISBN 9780811239462 (paperback) |
ISBN 9780811239479 (ebook)
Subjects: LCGFT: Novels.
Classification: LCC PT8176.13.H727 N3813 2025 |
DDC 839.813/74—dc23/eng/20241206
LC record available at https://lccn.loc.gov/2024058702

2 4 6 8 10 9 7 5 3 1

New Directions Books are published for James Laughlin
by New Directions Publishing Corporation
80 Eighth Avenue, New York 10011

Contents

Natalja's story about destiny

—There was once a woman who traveled all the way from Crimea to Denmark so that she could bury her mother.

That's how my grandmother always began the story of her life, for she loved to talk about herself in the third person as if it were something she had read about in a book rather than something she herself had experienced.

She was born in 1887 on the outskirts of St. Petersburg in a large wooden house with a veranda painted blue, and a garden leading straight down to the river to a small pier with a white pavilion.

The property was only open to the side facing the river; the other three sides were surrounded by a high garden wall, and all you could see were the tops of the fruit trees in the orchard.

But down in the village you could see the house's fruity towers, which at sunset looked golden and edible. And even though it was said that gold was poisonous, many were hungry enough to feel envious.

My grandmother grew up in that house as the only child of Alexander Firenko and his wife Marie, whom he had abducted from Copenhagen so as not to return to Russia empty-handed.

On his journey home from studying the silk trade in Marseille and Lyon for many years, he had decided to spend what was left of his money on making Marie his wife.

He had gone into a fabric store on the city's main street because he believed he could best assess a city and its people through something he knew. Here he noticed a young lady assessing the quality of the silk fabrics with a similar discernment. He approached her with a smile and gestures and not many words.

After giving a little lift to a roll of half silk, schappe, and bourette, she responded by spreading out the pure silk one so they could really sense the many millions of mulberry leaves eaten and transformed into this more imperishable fabric. It would take years to wear out and the threads to show through, the way in autumn you can see through the veins of leaves.

They both marveled at how the silk shimmered and draped, its mirror reversals from front to back between the matte and shiny side, and they carried it over to the window, in fact, they went outside, all the way out into the street, in order to judge its color in the daylight. Even though it was black, they both knew not all blacks are the same and that it would fade either toward brown or blue. And they preferred blue, because Marie had a wilderness of blue-black hair and skin with the same raw fineness of unglazed, factory-made porcelain.

—Where should we send it? asked the clerk, looking at Alexander Firenko, who pretended not to hear anything because he was lost in his thoughts.

—Thank you, but we'll take it with us, said Marie, picking up the package by the little wooden handle that the clerk had attached to the cord. Firenko got the bill and paid. And when they were standing out on the street, he took Marie's arm, pretending to lead her home. The next day they were married and on their way to St. Petersburg.

Marie had in fact led her Russian back home to Villa Elba, which bordered Frederiksberg Garden. It was autumn, and the garden path was covered in a dense carpet of wet leaves. Firenko could smell snow and thought that he would remember the leaves' colors and use them for a tablecloth made of silk. He would place that tablecloth on the veranda table, and on a high-backed chair he would place Marie,

3

and there she would sit embroidering all winter, and once in a while she would look down at the river that was frozen solid, and in the spring her longing would recede little by little. In the summer and autumn, she would consider herself lucky to have been abducted and destined for such a beautiful and peaceful life in the Russian countryside.

The Russian countryside. That was the expression my grandmother always used when she told her story.

—There was once a woman, she said, —who traveled all the way from Crimea to Denmark so that she could bury her mother. And she did it because back then her mother, who was named Marie, had been in great distress and therefore allowed herself to be abducted from Copenhagen by a lovestruck Russian who had taken her with him to the Russian countryside.

The fact that the abduction took place was the result of circumstances that my grandmother always called lucky, happy, and fruitful. For that evening when Marie led Alexander Firenko into Villa Elba, she was actually many weeks pregnant by a gardener from the Frederiksberg Garden.

He was called Long, not because he was especially tall, but because, overall, there was something elongated about him. Including his face and his nose, his arms, hands, and nails. Every inch of his body had the

4

same general elongated quality. But just as a weeping beech propagates in the same way as an ordinary beech, Long had the same effect on women as if he'd been tall and slender or, for that matter, short and compact. In fact, maybe his effect was even stronger because women were so unprepared for it and because his body over theirs felt like a protected space, similar to the cave found under the weeping beech's branches.

It was after her visits to that cave that Marie discovered she was expecting a child, who'd later become my grandmother, and who, on the very evening that Firenko traveled through Copenhagen, needed another father, in place of Long, who already had a wife and plenty of children.

When Marie bade her Russian guest into the living room of the Villa Elba, she intimated that her parents were not home.

She pointed to the large painting over the fireplace of General Theophil Petersen and his wife on a mountain trek in the Alps. It was her job as the housemaid to dust it off every morning so that the snow on the mountaintop would remain white. She thought it was lucky that she had the same last name as the general. Maybe she didn't need to ever tell Firenko that the wonderful couple with chins lifted toward the alpine sky were only her masters, whom she was forced to wait on hand and foot around the clock. Whereas her own parents were long dead and buried. No, she probably never had to tell Firenko, because he let her know with gestures and caresses that she looked exactly like her mother. The same pale skin, the same broad mouth, and the same blue-black silky hair. He ruffled it a bit and kissed her on the nose.

—And the next day they got married, added my grandmother always at this point in the story. —And soon after, they sailed to St. Petersburg, where Firenko's family, who belonged to the landed gentry, welcomed them warmly and gave them a large property on the outskirts of town. That's where their only daughter was born, in May of 1887, and they named her Natalja.

Gradually, as time went on, my grandmother embellished the story, and every time it was told, new details were added.

I imagine the past was becoming clearer for her because she was done thinking about the future. I also think that she finally gave up hiding things from me because she'd rather divulge them than take them to the grave.

Basically, it was as if she were trying to make her entire life disappear into the story. As if she thought it would be best to get it all out of her body before she died. But new riddles, new people and incidents, continued to surface, and so she had to keep beginning the story over again.

—There was once a woman named Natalja Alexandrovna who traveled all the way from Crimea to Denmark so that she could bury her mother. She did it because her mother, who grew up in a working-class family near Skive and was named Marie Petersen at her baptism, wished to be buried in the same place where she was born.

That's how my grandmother always began her story about how her world fell apart during the Russian Revolution and how she had to flee up through Europe to Copenhagen without bringing anything more than an old travel bag, which was made by Schwerin on Pile Street and which her mother had taken with her to St. Petersburg when she let herself be abducted by the young silk trader Alexander Firenko.

This travel bag for many years belonged to the general in whose house Marie had worked as a maid, General Theophil as he was always called, even though Theophil was just his first name. The bag was made to order for a handsome sum because it was an exact copy of a bag belonging to, by all accounts, Napoleon's deputy.

At least old Schwerin claimed that he had seen

the original at a private collector's in Paris and there was evidence that the bag had been on the Russian campaign.

The copy had now similarly traveled to Russia and back again. Although, without the same contents outbound as homebound.

During the last years of her life, my grandmother raved about all the treasures her mother and Firenko had taken with them in their travel bag when they left Villa Elba. First and foremost, the general's large coin collection, his pistols, and the bag of gold pieces he hid in his tobacco cabinet, along with an array of jewelry and silverware, and a Chinese crock, which Marie had cherished, one of those ordinary kinds with a lid, so useful in the household. A blue dragon twisted like a rootless tree across one side of it. Marie wrapped it in a piece of black silk, once purchased to sew a new blouse to wear while serving General Theophil's guests.

When my grandmother died, I inherited the rest of the General's treasures, his travel bag, and the piece of black silk, which my grandmother never had the heart to use.

The last time my grandmother told her life story, she began as she usually did.

—There was once a woman named Natalja who

traveled all the way from Crimea to Denmark so that she could bury her mother in the same place she was born.

And then she went on to talk about how Czar Nicholas II was overthrown and there was civil war and famine all over Russia. And how her father Alexander Firenko was one of the first to be killed because he didn't grasp what was happening.

—That woman named Natalja, said my grandmother, talking about herself, —was still unmarried when all these events unfolded, although she was over thirty. That was because her father wouldn't let her marry the forester in charge of the grove. His name was Boris and he came from one of the small brown wooden houses down in the village. Starting when he was a boy, he'd swim underwater to the small pier at the end of the garden to glimpse the large wooden house with many towers and a veranda painted blue. Natalja might've spotted him there and invited him up to the white pavilion. That's how they became secret lovers.

—But when the Firenko family's buildings and land holdings were confiscated, Natalja's childhood home was also lost, along with the forest and Boris, who, it was believed, had become deranged from his yearlong affair with Natalja—here my grandmother continued talking about herself in the third person—and he was forced to marry an older cousin.

At this time, it became urgent for Natalja and her mother to flee south with the White Guard. They only managed to pack the old travel bag with a few valuables and the most important family documents.

—And then my mother insisted on bringing her old Chinese crock, said my grandmother angrily. —It was filled with lard and wrapped carefully in a piece of black silk.

By the time the two women managed to reach Crimea, they had eaten all the lard, and most of their valuables had been used to pay for food and drink. All that was left was a pistol, a few pieces of jewelry, and a half dozen gold coins. They worked as nurses at a field hospital to make their supplies stretch a little longer. That's where her mother got sick and died from dysentery along with hundreds of others. In order to prevent the infection from spreading, the dead were all burned on bare ground. Natalja gathered up some of the ashes into the Chinese crock and started out on the long journey from Crimea to Denmark to bring her mother's earthly remains back to where she was born, even though these remains were now mixed with the remains of all the others; even though Natalja could not be sure if she managed to get any of her mother's ashes into the crock at all.

Along the way, she was often asked what was in the crock. Was it pickled ginger, or maybe blackberries with sugar and vodka, or was it sour cream, cheese, lard, or spices perhaps? Each time she laughed and said that it was a mix of everything.

She got in an accident on one of the many train lines. She had been sleeping for a long time and no longer knew where she was. Maybe in the Tatra Mountains, maybe somewhere else altogether. She asked the conductor where they were and if any trains went through the Tatra Mountains. He didn't answer. Suddenly, it was as if the earth had disappeared under the train. She was flung into the air, where it felt like she was floating for an eternity before falling and striking her head on something hard. But during that eternity, she thought she was on her way down into a tall fern from the past where a black snail was signaling for help with its antennae until the paramedics came.

When she awoke, she was told that someone had found her unconscious, clutching her travel bag like in sleep when you wrap your body around the blanket, protecting it, even though it should be the other way around. She couldn't remember anything. She couldn't even remember that her name was Natalja. The only thing she could think of was the burial and the crock with the mixed ashes representing her mother. But she didn't know where in the world she had landed, only that she now found herself in a room with seven people whom she'd never seen before. She sat upright in her chair, clutching the bag with the Chinese crock.

My grandmother couldn't grasp what was going on around her. She thought the funeral might be underway. And perhaps soon she would be asked to present the crock. She searched her memory for her mother's name. The priest was already deep into his sermon, and in a little while he would wave her over. She was afraid she wouldn't get up at the right moment, and so, to be safe, she took the crock out of her bag and kept it on her lap. She stared fixedly at the blue dragon twisting like a rootless tree on one side of it.

After a while, as her hands warmed the porcelain and she started to calm down, she was able to follow what was being said and understood that the voice speaking did not belong to a priest but an antiques dealer. She put the crock back in the bag. She didn't want him to think that she wanted to sell it.

Then, she realized that in a moment it would be her turn to speak. She couldn't possibly remember anything. But, in fact, she knew a great deal by heart. And so, it was probably best that she started from the beginning.

—There was once a woman who traveled all the way from Crimea to Denmark so that she could bury her mother.

Then the rest would surely follow, and before she knew it, she would have arrived at the end.

Natalja's story about the murder

It was last summer when you couldn't get more than a few feet from home before it started to rain. One day I made it all the way to the café by the mailbox, or, more precisely, under the portal across the street, before it began to pour.

The square looked like the bottom of a well filling up. All around in alcoves along the slimy walls were small flocks of people pressed together, waiting for the water to rise.

Out in the rain the acacias' supple branches were moving like flowing seaweed and the birds had already learned to swim.

A street sweeper said he thought all the rain was caused by pollution.

A housewife sticking her head out the window beside the portal said it was a bad omen when her cat refused to eat liver. In one of his past lives, he'd been a priest who made predictions from the livers of different animals, birds, and yes, even people. So, she just wanted to warn us that at any second we were going to be swept away by a torrent and all its sludge and vegetable scraps from the market, and we should not think that in the end we'd fare any better than a leek top or a rotten lemon on our way to the realm of the dead.

Most of the flock smiled vaguely, staring out over the square like when you're standing in line at the butcher's and one of the customers suddenly starts complaining that there's something wrong with the meat, but, fortunately, there are other butchers.

For once, I'm on my way to another butcher shop I only know about because its name is on the plastic bag I'm carrying. Not because I don't like my own butcher. He's always fair and there are never any problems. But I'm curious to see what it's like at this other place.

It's all because of the plastic bag. Otherwise, I never would've gone out. It was on Badinot's kitchen counter in the morning when I stopped by to feed the cat.

The calm, slightly solemn cat is named Mirage. She's black with a reddish-brown tinge and eyes of different colors. One is a radiant blue and seems blind, the other is dark and only visible as a glimmer in the fur. Still, she's a very concentrated cat. When I came in, for example, she was already poised on the kitchen chair as if she were about to eat with a fork and knife.

There was no food to be found anywhere, however. Badinot didn't have a refrigerator, but would shop every day. Which he obviously hadn't done. The plastic bag had been placed on the counter so I could see where he usually shopped. And that was all the way down by the Seine on one of the long side streets I didn't know. Surely a butcher was there who knew all about Mirage.

I gave her what I could find from my own refrigerator, took the plastic bag, and hurried out while the weather was still dry.

But, as I said, I only make it to the portal across from the café when it starts to pour again. When the housewife in the window starts going on about our arrival to the land of the dead with rotten lemons, I get tired of waiting. I take off my blue sandals, put them in the plastic bag, and press them against my chest. Then I run across the street in my bare feet. The water comes up to my ankles, and the raindrops bounce so high from the asphalt that they splash under my dress. My dress is already soaked and clinging to my body in the short time it takes to reach the café. Inside, a thick steam hangs in the air from all the wet clothes, and the voices sound like a tropical hum.

I squeeze myself down at a table facing the street. A young woman on her way home from playing tennis lends me her hand towel. It smells like dirt. It's late morning and it seems like twilight sinks around us. Now it's raining so hard that the cars pull over and wait. I see a man edge out with a briefcase on his head like a waiter with an empty tray. Over at the counter, the Black man, who is in love, is having another glass of beer, waiting for his girlfriend. He always keeps his hat on. It's a pith helmet of burgundy-colored felt, which he usually pushes over his eyes so that he looks like a police officer who's sleeping standing up. But now, his eyes are what's shining most brightly in the whole square.

I get up and go over to buy cigarettes. People come streaming in from the parked cars and shake more rain off themselves. Umbrellas hang and drip from the counter. I'm still barefoot. As I'm standing there with the cigarettes in my hand, I suddenly hear myself asking for a pad of paper and a pen. I sense people are staring at me. An envelope and a stamp, I add, and pay.

I'm sitting here at my table with a cup of coffee that's nearly empty. I'm not writing a letter, because I don't know anyone to whom I can write. Yet, I don't want people to think I have nothing to write about, and so I just write. Quietly and calmly. Without interruption.

Once I saw a young woman writing a letter in this

way. On a train going through Belgium. And when she was done, she folded all the sheets of paper and slid them inside an envelope without even glancing at what she'd written. What if she forgot to mail it? What if the recipient rejected it or ripped it up? Never think so far ahead, I tell myself as I'm writing, because so much is only read once as it's being written.

I've never set out to write anything before. It must have something to do with the tightly packed room, the atmosphere of thick steam coming off all the creatures washed ashore into this café, now chatting and laughing so that their voices remain in the air. It's as calming as the rain's violent sound, drowning out my sentences, making me unafraid to write them.

It gradually dawns on me that there's nothing to be afraid of, since what arises almost automatically as I write is my grandmother's story, which she's told me so many times that I can nearly recite it by heart.

Perhaps the rain and the acacias' underwater movements remind me of the cloudbursts and landslides that my grandmother encountered in the Tatra Mountains when her train crashed. In any event, I write about how she ends up in a stalactite cave with seven people she's never met before but whom she now considers her closest relatives. And how the only thing she's saved is an old bag and a small Chinese crock with a lid, now being used as her mother's urn, which she promised to bring all the way from Crimea to Copenhagen.

And, as I'm thinking about how things went for her in Copenhagen, I lift my gaze half inwardly so that I both see and don't see a monk crossing the square, moving in a peculiar way, as if he's moving the rain in a column along with him inside the rain.

I only know one person who moves like that and before thinking about it, I tear open the café door and yell—Jacques! so loudly that everyone in the café is silent for a moment, staring out at the monk, who turns and looks right at me, and I know it's Jacques, my beloved Jacques, and for a second I can tell he recognizes me, but in the next moment, he acts as though he's never seen me before and so he never really stops, but just continues on with his column of rain.

I hurry back to my table, grab my purse, pay, and leave. Fortunately, the voices around me quickly pick up again. Especially when the Black man's girlfriend arrives at the same time but instead of entering right away, she positions herself in the middle of the square in the middle of the rain, standing there like a plant that can't get enough water. Her boyfriend watches her proudly. Until she starts to dance around with arms lifted high and waving, and he realizes she's no child. He runs out with an umbrella and brings her inside.

I pay and go downstairs to the bathroom. I look at myself in the mirror, as if to see why Jacques didn't recognize me. The blue-black hair, which he loves, the thick eyebrows, the white skin and thick irregular lips. Why was he disguised as a monk? And why do we always meet at his place? Why do I always have to go to him, all the way to the other side of Buttes Chaumont; why does he never come down here to my neighborhood, not once? When I asked him, he simply answered, It's better that way. He's the same age as my parents. I decide I will call him as soon as I get home. I also consider going and talking to my mother, but I haven't even told her about him. And I never see my father. He sends me two pairs of shoes for Christmas, and two for my birthday. They don't always fit, but I never send them back. His factory isn't doing so well, and my mother complains that she never receives her money.

When I get back upstairs, the rain has stopped and most of the patrons have hurried off. It's almost as if the monk had never walked by, and especially not in the form of Jacques. But as I'm walking out, I hear the manager shout to the waiter who's drying the floor: — We haven't seen that Albanian monk for a long time!

—Yeah, didn't he just walk by? She yelled Jacques. But that's not his name.

—They say he has a wife in every neighborhood and everywhere he's got another name. Damn shame for that little pale woman.

They can't see me because I'm exiting through the side door. The Albanian monk. Well, they can all call themselves Albanians then. That little pale woman. There's no way I'll ever set foot in there again.

I'm freezing and don't care if my blue shoes get ruined. I run through the puddles, dying to get home to Mirage to feed her. As I'm running, I check on the butcher's street number. 72. I stop when I reach the street because most of the buildings have been torn down and I see no shops at all.

I walk down the street anyway until I see number 72 over on the other side. If you didn't know better, you wouldn't be able to tell if this house was the only one ever built on the street or the only one left standing. That's how melancholy it looks.

On the stairs, a North African boy is scratching the wall with a simple knife. Beside him is a small, thin-legged dog of the black-white variety that leaves the impression that all dogs have the same name.

I remind myself I've only come here because I expected to find a butcher shop. On the wall you can see some letters remaining that match the advertising on the plastic bag, but the windows are shuttered and the shop is closed.

Now the dog comes toward me and I notice that I'm afraid of both the dog and the knife. Yet, I am even more afraid of turning my back, and so I slowly cross the street, appearing to be checking out the boy's series of scratches on the wall.

—What are you staring at? he asks.

—Who are you asking for?

—The police.

—Really, is that who told you to stand here?

—Yeah.

—When did they tell you?

—When they were leaving.

—How long do you have to stand here?

—I don't know. Until they pick the body up, I guess. That probably won't happen until dark.

I'm just about to join his little game when I hear knocking coming from inside the building. I move in the direction of the door.

—It's no use, it's locked, the boy says.

—Yeah, but, someone inside knocked, I say. —The person who knocked might open the door for us.

—No, he can't, says the boy all-knowingly. —It's just Badinot, and he doesn't have a key.

—Badinot, I say.

—Yeah, the two police officers forced him in there. They shoved a gun in his back and forced him into the building.

—Badinot, I say again. —Where did you get that name from?

—From Badinot. Where else would I get it?

—What does he look like?

—Normal.

—How normal? What was he wearing?

—He always wears a cap. And, uh, he has a small, brown schoolbag that he always uses, even though he's a grown-up.

—That's Badinot, I say.

—That's just what I said. They forced him in there, even though he fought them. And a little later there was a shot. But they said Badinot wasn't the one who was dead. They said this when they were leaving.

—You know what, I said, —don't you think it's a shame for Badinot to be locked in there for so long? If you stay here, I'll run over to the police and ask them to come back sooner. Maybe they've forgotten.

—They usually never forget, he says. —But just go see.

I start walking and the dog follows me.

—Cachou, come here, the boy says.

I turn around. —I'll be right back, I say, waving.

Then I start to run as fast as I can. I burst into the café, and the manager stares at me as if the Albanian monk is on my tail.

—The police, I say. —Call the police. Badinot is being held hostage.

Badinot is one of the regulars, but still the manager just keeps staring at me, as if the Albanian monk has brainwashed me to lure him into a trap.

I grab the phone and dial the police myself, breathing in deeply and listening to my calm voice. —It concerns a child, I say. —Yes, in 72. His father is being held captive in the building, it's urgent. Yes, I'll go back there now.

The police have already arrived by the time I get back. The squad car is parked outside and Cachou is sitting on the steps. He follows me inside where I immediately run into Badinot.

—Don't go in any farther, he says.

—What happened? I ask.

—Is this your wife? the police officer asks.

—Yes, says Badinot.

I don't dare to disagree.

—Get that dog out of here, says one of the officers. —It'll destroy the tracks.

—Your husband is charged with murder, says the other one.

—You'd better follow us to the station.

—Murder, I say.

—Yeah, the Albanian monk is dead, says the North African boy. —It doesn't matter.

—Don't say that, Badinot says as I push the officer aside and go into the other room.

There's a desk, a bed, and some chairs. Oh, Mirage. There's just no butcher shop. Lying there on the bed is the monk, the Albanian monk, as they call him, but I call him Jacques. The boy has taken my hand and I stifle my cries. I step closer to see his wonderful face. It's closed and hard as rock, and I can't believe that I've ever known him.

Still, I bend down to touch his hair. I close my eyes and lift it a little. I weigh it in my hand. It's as heavy as silk. I just stand there with it in my hand to remember him as he was. Then I open my eyes.

But instead of letting go of his hair, I pull it toward me because in the place where the hair would otherwise lay spread out, I see the corpse of my father, my dead father's face, and he looks like when I used to watch him sleeping when I was a child. And I faint.

The first thing I see when I wake up is Cachou. The dog is lying on the rug with my purse between his paws. Mirage and the North African boy are at the table; Mirage has a large serving of liver in front of her. I'm lying in Badinot's bed because until he gets out of prison I will act as his wife—and no one knows if this will continue once he gets back home. In any case, now I'm caring for the boy, who calls himself Amman. For the first time in a long time I'm happy to be alive. I think we will make it. I've got a job down at the café. And Amman helps with the cleaning after we close.

—The riddle is solved, says Amman.

He loves to repeat the whole story.

—But there are other riddles, he adds. —Do you want to hear them?

Then I have to listen to what he's written.

—At 8:45 a.m., two men break into Badinot's apartment. They're dressed as cops and they force Badinot to go with them down to the butcher's shop. He manages to put out the plastic bag, hoping you'll figure out where he is. Down in the shop they order Badinot to shoot your father. What's his name again?

—Eugène Valadon.

—We just called him the boss. Badinot was his courier and I helped him. Have you examined the blue shoes you ruined in the rain; maybe there's heroin in them, or diamonds.

I shake my head no.

He takes them out and slices them up with his knife but finds nothing.

—Yeah, but when Badinot fires his shot, he says,

—the boss is already dead. That Albanian monk has killed him and is bending over him, so when Badinot shoots, he kills the monk. The monk was an amazing courier. No one ever suspected him. I'd like to be a monk!

When Amman and Cachou have fallen asleep and Mirage is shut out on the sloping roof in front of the window, I write my questions down.

How did I fall in love with a man who could dress as a monk and kill my father? Why did I do everything he asked? And why do I align my destiny with the man who killed him even if it was only by mistake?

I'm sitting here staring at the small chunks of liver Mirage didn't eat as the rain picks up again. As the sound of rain grows constant, I continue to write my grandmother's story.

Natalja's story about the meeting

My grandmother was a real psychic.

Once, when I visited her near the end, when she was living on Gothers Road, she kept saying how amazing it was that I had traveled all the way from Paris to Copenhagen by myself when I was only twelve years old, and that my mother could never have made such a journey at that age, or even later, because that's how it is with such things, always skipping a generation, and then it emerges as something exceptional, as if occurring for the first time in the world.

—That's how mystery works, she whispered lowering her head, as if afraid the higher powers might hear that she knew what they were up to.

—What mystery? I asked.

—I'll tell you, she said, pulling me over to the dresser.

—Imagine one day you're found unconscious, and you can't remember anything. You can't even remember your name is Natalja. You don't know where you are, only that you've ended up in a room with seven people you've never seen before. You sit up tall in your chair clutching your travel bag. Inside it is this Chinese crock that's right here.

She pointed to it and then turned it a little so I could see the blue dragon twisting like a rootless tree on one side of it.

I stared at it hard.

—Here's how it'll go, she whispered secretively, —here's how it'll go. In the crock you will have your mother's ashes, which you must promise to bring back to Denmark so she can be buried in the same place where she was born.

I promised, the way you promise something you don't expect will ever be necessary to fulfill.

—Nothing you need to be afraid of, said my grandmother, kissing me on the forehead.

—I myself have had my mother's ashes in that very crock. I think I sat with it on my lap the whole way from Crimea to the graveyard over in North Jutland, a place near Skive, where my mother was to be buried.

—So, when it's your turn, she concluded, —remember that I at that time escaped alive.

—I will, I said. But I dared not ask why the Chinese crock was sitting on the dresser in Copenhagen when it should in fact be buried in a graveyard in Jutland.

—I know what you're thinking, my grandmother said then.

She was indeed psychic, for not only could she see into the future, and similarly into the past, she could also see straight through someone, so nothing was hidden from her, and that's how it was with everyone she met.

—You're worried that the crock has been filled in advance, she continued calmly, —but it hasn't, it's empty.

—See for yourself, she said opening it and blowing into it.

Indeed, there was nothing to see.

—And do you know why it's empty?

I shook my head. I didn't want to tell her I believed in resurrection.

—It's because the first thing the priest said when I placed the Chinese crock on his desk was that he never buried people in anything other than coffins. Even though I explained how far I'd traveled and all that had happened, he wouldn't budge: I had to get a coffin.

—I bought it with the last of my money, which only covered a child's coffin. The ashes were poured in and the lid was nailed shut. It was a little wooden coffin. They placed it in her parents' grave site. The next day I returned with a small boulder with her name on it—Marie, it read in tarred letters.

—Do you know how I got hold of that? she asked.

—You stole it, I whispered.

—No, I made it myself, she said proudly. —After saying goodbye to the priest, I passed a road crew. There I found a stone and asked if I could dip my stick in the melted tar to write on it.

—The next day when the letters were dry, I carried it over to the grave site. I knew very well that only children's graves have stones with just the first name, but there was no space for anything else. So now it seems as if she never left the village she grew up in because she wasn't very old when she died.

—Actually, she lived to be over sixty and early in her life had allowed herself to be abducted by a Russian silk trader and brought to Leningrad, where she gave birth to me and from there we were later forced to flee to Crimea.

—We only managed to pack that old travel bag with some valuables and the most important family papers.

—But then my mother insisted on bringing her old Chinese crock. It was filled with lard and carefully wrapped in a piece of black silk, concluded my grandmother.

—Look at this, she said, lifting the lid of the crock.

—The fat was boiling hot when it was poured in. That's how it got all crackly, and the fat seeped in and created that discoloration.

—Smell it; it still smells rancid. She stuck the crock under my nose.

I couldn't smell anything. At least not fat. Of course, it had been nearly fifty years. Maybe it smelled a little like tea, but my grandmother probably couldn't remember what it had been used for all this time.

So that summer I went home with the crock, but I never showed it to my mother.

From then on, every time we met, my grandmother's plans for my future became more far-reaching. And I got completely engrossed in her stories about how I would live out my life. Which husband and family I would have. Which animals, birds, and plants I would love. Which house would eventually be mine. A large wooden house with a veranda painted blue, and a garden leading straight down to the river, my grandmother said dreamily, to the small pier with the white pavilion.

At the time, I regarded it all as a game we shared. A game that enabled my grandmother to dip back into childhood and tell about the house in Russia she grew up in, speaking about it as though it had found itself somewhere out in the future.

But what once seemed like a game has since proven to be deadly serious. Not that I live or ever lived in that Russian house. In any case, not yet.

But I have met the exact man my grandmother warned me about, although I didn't know it was him until after he died.

One day, when we were looking at the family album, my eye caught a photo of a young man posing near a car. Taken in the 1930s. His head was bare and he had a piercing gaze; his mouth had a little self-absorbed smile that seemed seductive.

—He's someone I could fall in love with, I said laughing.

My grandmother made the sign of the cross and mumbled a prayer in Russian.

Then she went over and opened one of the dresser drawers.

She returned to the table with a square package about the size of an ordinary cutting board. It was wrapped in black silk and bound with what seemed like strips of bridal-veil lace.

My grandmother placed it between us, laying her hand on it as if to drive it away.

—Inside this package, she said slowly, —is an old mirror with a frightening quality. If you look at your reflection, your face will be missing.

—I was given this mirror long ago by that man in the picture, the one you thought you could fall in love with. His name is Viktor Blanke. He is the devil himself. And the day you meet him and fall instantly in love with him, it's best that you have the mirror and that you turn it toward him.

—But why would I meet him, I objected. —He must be over on the other side of the mountains, or, when did you see him last?

—That's right, he's over on the other side of the mountains, said my grandmother. —But believe me, you'll meet him.

I thought she was looking rather vengeful, so I picked a little at the lace strips.

—You definitely must not open this before it's time, she said.

—Please tell me how you got this mirror, I said, pushing the package a little to the side.

—It was when we had our first antique shop. One afternoon, I was alone in the store and he came in with a mirror under his arm and set it down on the counter with the backside up.

—As soon as he walked in I fell in love with him, even though he was only nineteen and I was over forty.

—Before I knew it, we were lying together on an old mahogany bed in the back of the store.

—Afterwards, he gave me the mirror, stressing that I must only look at it after he was dead, otherwise my face would be missing. I shuddered at the thought and hid it in a drawer between my undergarments.

—He came almost every day for several months, but suddenly one day he stopped coming, and, even though I missed him, I quickly got used to ordinary life again. I was of course an old married woman after all, a busy housewife, and Constance, your mother, was still living at home. Her father spoiled her and she was allowed to do far too much.

—And so, I had almost forgotten about Viktor Blanke, when suddenly one day he walks into the shop with Constance and it's clear she's wildly in love with him.

—Full of sorrow, shame, and rage, I felt like sinking into the earth.

—Constance introduces him to me, and I'm forced to pretend that I'd never set eyes on him before.

—I remember the mirror and sincerely wish that he would die then and there, but nothing happens.

—For months I have to keep up the charade. I know he's an impostor, but I can't prove it to either Constance or her father. Karl has never been particularly gullible, but Viktor immediately wins him over and they enter into business agreements, and a wedding is soon on its way.

—What in the world should I do? In the end, I fetched my last gold coins. The ones my mother stole from her masters when she fled to Russia. Although stole isn't the right word of course. Because in fact she had to fool her silk trader into believing that the masters were her parents and that the gold coins were money she was borrowing from her future inheritance.

—That silk trader, my dear father, Alexander Firenko—(suddenly my grandmother looked as round and Russian as an onion dome)—he never harbored the least suspicion about my mother, and the coins were stowed away, only to be used in case of a dire emergency.

—Only a few were used now and then over the years. But enough were still left to fend off the dangerous situation that my family and I, and especially my beloved little Constance, now found ourselves in.

—With the remaining Copenhagen gold, as my mother always called it, I hired a detective who could quickly provide evidence that the icons Viktor Blanke had procured for us and many others were forgeries he'd made himself.

—Karl of course wanted him to be punished, but for Constance's sake, and in large part, my own, I would rather have him out of the country once and for all.

—And that's what we paid him for, with our entire savings.

—On top of everything, Constance ran away from home when she heard Viktor was gone.

—This was just before the war, and I didn't see her again until the beginning of the fifties. By then she was long since married to the manufacturer and was called Madame Valadon. When I asked her if in all that time she had seen anything of Viktor, she said no, she had not. But I still don't know whether my little Constance was telling the truth. Because that devil pops up everywhere, whispered my grandmother, looking at me with squinting eyes.

I kept quiet and thought about my mother, who was detained in Paris during the Second World War and who, because of all these circumstances, had been too proud to return home.

—And so, one evening when a friend invited her to a gathering, she made up her mind beforehand that she would marry the first most eligible man.

—She spotted him as soon as she walked in. He was standing over by the fireplace, where, on the mantle, he had placed a row of shoes and he was turning and twisting and showing them off.

That's the one, thought my mother, and went right over and listened patiently to him talking all about shoes and made up her mind on the spot never to be separated from him no matter what happened. I always imagined that she was motivated by the fact that she was in need of a new pair of shoes. But, in any case, that's how she got married, feeling that she had also taken revenge on Viktor Blanke, who had failed her by accepting the bribe to go away.

—Maybe you could check the mirror to see if he's alive, I said to my grandmother.

—No, now it's time to go to bed, she said, shaking her head, as if I had been entertaining her for far too long with something we shouldn't be speaking about.

— When you leave tomorrow, you will take the mirror with you for safety's sake.

Late at night, when I was lying in bed thinking about my grandmother's story about the mirror, I suddenly heard a long drawn-out cry from the dining room. I rushed in and there was my grandmother standing in the middle of the room clutching the mirror to her chest.

—He's alive, she whimpered. —He's alive. And my face, it's not there.

It was difficult to calm her down. She was clutching the mirror so hard that I couldn't loosen her fingers.

—Let me look, I said. —Let me look in the mirror, let me look and see if I'm also not there.

—Don't touch it, said my grandmother. She suddenly became completely calm and began wrapping up the mirror again. —I forbid you to touch it before he's dead.

Her voice was so strange that I knew obeying her was a matter of life and death.

—At least *I* can still see your face, I said to comfort her.

My grandmother lifted her hands and slid her fingers down over her cheeks to her mouth.

—It's returned, she said. —When I looked at myself in the mirror there was nothing there. My face was missing. But that's not even the worst of it. The worst was when I lifted my hand without thinking to feel my face and I couldn't feel anything. My fingers disappeared into thin air. That's why I screamed.

Her eyes were filling with tears and she wiped them away. Now that she was sure that her face was there again, she laughed out loud.

I don't know if it had anything to do with that experience, but shortly after, my grandmother died.

The mirror has been stored along with my other Danish keepsakes for many years.

Not until recently had it seen the light of day. One day when I got home, Amman, whom I've adopted, was playing with it.

—Get away from that! I shouted.

—What is it? he asked calmly.

—A mirror! I shouted, lunging for him.

He turned the mirror toward me. —Then look at yourself, if you can! he yelled.

I closed my eyes and cried. I felt blind.

—It's just an ordinary Madonna, said Amman, putting his arm around me.

Later, it would turn out that he was right. It was a Madonna, but she was not so ordinary. I found out that she was called the Albanian Madonna. And, as the story goes, she moved her image from mirror to mirror as soon as one of her persecutors died.

Now I understood that the man I'd been in love with, whom I lived and breathed for, had been the Madonna's last persecutor; Viktor Blanke, who'd made a living forging icons most of his life, was at last dead. He told me his name was simply Jacques, and people in the neighborhood never called him anything other than the Albanian monk, but in my heart, I always knew he was the devil himself.

Natalja's story about getting lost

The family was always getting lost. But not me.

It wasn't until that trip when I got in a train accident and apparently forgot everything that I started to believe I would finally realize the family dream of getting really lost. But no. It wasn't going to be so easy. More on that later.

For most of the family it happens on its own accord. One day they're suddenly so far from home that they don't know where they are. But that never happens to me. No matter how far and wide I roam, I always know exactly where I am and how to find my way back to the starting point.

And so, I was never one of those small children in the family who fell in the river and got fished out or who outright drowned in a water hole and became an example of the family's dangerous desire for adventure. Neither will I, in due time, be one of the elders who, taken by surprise by the dark, lies down to die in a shed or forest where there is shelter. Even though I might wish it would end up like that for me.

I've often thought that maybe by mimicking one of the family stories, I could outwit my own sense of direction and get even more lost than my ancestors.

But most of the stories in their original form are not really suitable for replication. Especially if you want to do something more extreme than what's already been done in most of the family's stories.

I'll just mention the story about my grandmother's aunt, who, when her husband died, could not bear to be alone with him in the house, and so immediately got one of the coffins down from the attic, placed him in it, and rode up to the churchyard, despite the snowstorm that had been raging for several hours and having to first shovel the path to get the wagon out.

The next day she was found dead, buried in snow, far off on the other side of the church, where the wagon was stuck in house-high drifts.

When they were digging out the wagon, a sound came from inside the coffin, a moan from the man whose heart had begun to beat again from the rough handling when his wife dragged him into the coffin. When he woke up and saw the coffin lid above him, he didn't think, as most would in his situation, that he was buried alive, but that he, fully deserving of it, had been resurrected from the dead and was now lying there waiting for the light of Paradise to burst forth.

When at last he heard voices, he began shouting as if he'd lost all his senses, suddenly overjoyed by the thought that now he would meet everyone who had died before him.

That's why he was disappointed when they opened the lid and he saw that it was only the people from the village, people he'd known for many years and every single day had spoken to about the weather and whatever else was happening.

And even though everyone told him that he had been granted a new life, it seemed as if he couldn't enjoy it. Every time there was a snowstorm, he'd hitch up and ride off, but he never got lost any more like he did that day in the coffin, and everything was simply a matter of course.

There is something about only being able to get lost when you're not thinking about it. It requires a certain talent that I don't have at all. That's why I've also had to rely on luck, and I truly believed it came to my rescue during the journey to bring my mother's ashes from Paris to Copenhagen when the train I was on suddenly crashed.

I had been asleep for a long time and no longer knew where I was. Maybe in the Tatra Mountains. Even though I had no idea where the Tatra Mountains were. Even though, if I thought about it, I knew perfectly well that the only mountains the train was going to cross were the Ardennes. In any case, I asked the conductor where we were and if there was a train that passed through the Tatra Mountains. He didn't answer because suddenly it was as if the earth had disappeared from under the train and I was flung into the air, where it felt like I was floating for an eternity before falling and striking my head on something hard.

When I awoke, I was told that someone had found me unconscious still clutching my travel bag like in sleep when you wrap your body around the blanket, protecting it, even though it should be the other way around. I couldn't remember anything. I couldn't even remember that my name was Natalja. Natalja Valadon. The only thing I could think about was the burial and the crock with the mixed ashes representing my mother.

Now, it's all too clear to me. First and foremost, the image of my mother's gruesome death in the flames. But also, the mysterious image of my father, Eugène Valadon, who was murdered by my mother's lover, Viktor Blanke, who, again, admittedly by mistake, murdered my father in the same moment he himself was murdered by my friend Badinot, actually by his two buddies dressed as cops, who were forced to murder my father in revenge for the entire cartel that he'd been running with an iron fist.

My father's burial went according to plan even though my mother and I always get lost in Montmartre's cemetery paths.

—The funeral procession was just as large as if he'd died a natural death, my mother said.

She seemed so resolute. I thought she could easily start a new life because, even though they'd lived apart for many years, my father's existence had still loomed over her like a shadow, all because she had decided early on never to divorce him.

But Viktor Blanke's burial on the other hand ended with my mother's horrific suicide.

Without my knowledge, he'd been my mother's lover for several years, and during that time he'd become mine, without my awareness of his having any name other than Jacques.

It only dawned on me later that Viktor Blanke, alias Jacques, lived a double life.

And yet at the funeral I had no idea that my mother had known him. She never showed any signs, and I experienced only her support for me when I was completely out of my mind with grief and barely knew where I was or what I was doing.

That's why, after the short sermon in the chapel, I reluctantly agreed to all of us going down to the basement where we could attend the actual cremation, so I could see for myself that it really was my beloved

Jacques, alias Viktor Blanke, in his coffin being consumed by flames.

We stood there facing the oven. My mother asked if it was the right coffin because there were so many of them around. And even though the employee said that it was against regulations, he opened the coffin anyway so I could see who it was. When I saw him, I couldn't believe that I had ever loved him. Then when the employee opened the oven door and pushed the coffin inside, I stood there petrified and cold even though the heat was hitting me like a wall.

That's why it seemed like something from a movie when my mother let out an insane cry and threw herself into the roaring oven, and the terrified employee, who'd come rushing over, stood there for a moment with one of her shoes in his hand, before throwing it into the fire, closing the oven door, and fainting.

I didn't cry at all, but hurried to get a pitcher of water, which I poured over the employee.

When he came to, he said he was afraid he'd be accused of pushing my mother into the oven. I reassured him that my mother had thrown herself into the flames. And I knew it without even really having seen it. And, at the same time, I knew at once that she'd done it because she wanted to be united in death with the man she'd always loved. This insight was confirmed later when I went through my mother's papers. Her sweetheart from before had returned. And, luckily, she had no idea about his relationship to me.

Therefore, I'm not only bringing my mother's ashes back; they're mixed with the ashes of Viktor Blanke, alias Jacques, my once much-beloved Jacques.

Who, by the way, started out long ago by seducing my grandmother. But that's an old story.

I wish I could ask my grandmother for advice. She's the one I promised to bring my mother's ashes back to where she was born. Maybe she'd look at it differently now if she had the whole picture. Maybe she'd think that I should sprinkle the ashes into the sea and take the empty crock back with me, not because I'm afraid of ghosts or that the dead won't be able to rest in an ordinary grave. But in our family, there are people who get lost long after they're dead.

It's said that it goes all the way back to our Jutlandic past, to a summer day hundreds of years ago when our first ancestor that we're aware of, a philosophical shoemaker by the name of Hans Petersen, took his life by hanging himself on the village's gallows hill.

He hanged there for over a week before the executioner and his assistant went out to inspect The Place, as they called it.

—There you go, said the executioner, —he got it in the end, always bragging he could climb up any old tree no matter how slippery the trunk was.

And the assistant agreed that it was especially blasphemous when people hanged themselves where it was usually done by professionals.

Back then, a suicide couldn't be buried on consecrated ground; therefore, it was customary to place the coffin in a hay wagon, pulled by a pair of oxen, and to send the wagon out of the village without any driver other than the dead.

Then they'd pray that the oxen would find a place for the dead to rest. Everyone agreed the best thing that could happen was that the Romani would capture the stray cattle, bury the dead, sing for him, and, as payment, they could keep both oxen and wagon. This way everyone would know where the evil was located.

But that day when the dead shoemaker was the coachman, the oxen got lost in the bog and drowned, pulling the wagon with them into the deep water. Only the coffin broke free, resting on a little grassy islet surrounded by water on all sides. That's where it was found, a month later, already overgrown with plants, and people noticed that a little willow tree growing on the islet had branches in the shape of a cross.

Some believed that the suicide had risen up from

his coffin and planted the willow, twisting its branches as a sign. They had in fact seen him roaming around the area, looking in through someone's window, and then a little later in another one as people were sitting around the table eating. He was even seen in the church at a funeral, and people were afraid he'd slip into the coffin of one of the ordinary dead. Or that he'd take possession of the priest and transform him into a devil.

They'd seen that happen before. That's why they began making donations to his bereaved and placed a stone with his name on the family grave. So that he could sneak into it from time to time.

I once told this story to Viktor Blanke, who called himself Jacques.

He said it was incredible how long a person, dead or alive, could hide out in a village and still be part of the village's life.

He'd experienced it himself in the Balkans, where he lived in a small mountain village during the Second World War, a place that bordered Albania, Greece, and Macedonia.

How he ended up there he wouldn't say exactly. This was before I knew he was the one who gave my grandmother the mirror that later turned out to be a forged icon.

That's when I told him I'd once heard about the Albanian Madonna. As the story went, she moved her image from mirror to mirror as soon as one of her pursuers died.

—That story has certainly made its rounds, he said laughing. —Actually, it's a story about an ordinary Albanian girl who was clever enough to escape the Germans even though they'd trapped her. They chased her up to the church door and saw her run in, but still they couldn't find her.

—Why not, I asked. —I've seen pictures of churches in the Balkans and they're always so small.

—Perhaps you're familiar with those icons, Viktor Blanke replied. —They're sculpted from gold or silver, and the precious metal forms the Madonna's veil, hair, and halo, like a brilliant frame around an oval opening meant for her face painted on wood or canvas, which is sometimes replaced.

—It's said that the young woman hid herself by inserting her beautiful face in one after another of these empty oval frames in place of the images that were in the process of being painted, until she reached the back wall of the cabinet-like iconostasis, where she hid in the oval usually framing the holy Madonna. They never found her and so she was saved.

Viktor Blanke looked like he had dreamed himself back to the past, and I asked him what he'd done during that time among people whose language he had only learned little by little.

—I learned to paint icons, he said. —And then I learned a lot about getting lost in the right way, at the right time.

Of course he needed to explain this.

—Well, at one point, a rumor was going around in the village that the Germans were approaching, and they had already murdered all the men in other areas, except the oldest ones, or, in any case, they took them away.

—Our village was already occupied by the Italians whom we were living with day in and day out, and their ability to completely forget the war had almost rubbed off on us.

—We didn't want to lose this way of life. And so, I and all the local men dressed up as priests and monks, and when the Germans arrived, I was the one who spoke, explaining that all of my monks belonged to an order that took a vow of silence, and when we were fleeing we got lost in the forest near the border and asked them how we might now find our way back to our monastery.

—They asked us to describe where it was located, and a platoon followed us up over the mountains in the direction of the border.

—After a long time of wandering around in silence,

we stood in the middle of the forest in the densest wilderness I have ever seen, and one of the Germans pointed to a little pole and said there was the border. We should just walk in that direction and soon we'd be home.

—We wandered for hours and days without coming across any vestiges of anything. What began with pretending we were lost ended after a few days with us actually being so completely lost that we couldn't find our way back again.

That's why it ended as it did, and we were forced to call a random place, high in the desolate mountains, our home. There we built and furnished a monastery-like village in a clearing. The sheep that wandered in, we captured and retained. We surely would've done the same with the women, but none came. After the war, these "monks" were reunited with their wives down in the original village. I stayed up in the forest monastery for one more year before I traveled to Paris with my treasure of icons.

Here Viktor Blanke, alias Jacques, ended his story.

For a moment I thought he'd reignited my hope of getting lost.

But after his death, and after the death of my parents, I realized that for a long time I might've been lost without noticing it.

Why would I otherwise spend endless hours recalling my grandmother's plans for my future, which became more extensive each time we met? Why would I otherwise be so completely engulfed by her stories about how I would carry out my life? The man and family I'd have. The animals and birds and plants I'd love. The house that would one day be mine. A large wooden house with a veranda painted blue, and a garden leading straight down to the river, my grandmother saying it so dreamily, right down to the small pier with the white pavilion.

Natalja's story about liquor

There once was a cat named Mirage. That's more or less how I thought I would begin my story. Now of course you can say it's already begun as I thought it would—there once was a cat named Mirage and so on—whatever I can come up with now doesn't matter because it would be just one of countless but similar false beginnings. And if it had been a true beginning I would not have noticed it, would not have mistrusted it, I would not have ceased its development, and so on.

But why hide the fact that only Mirage the cat holds the big picture of this story and thereby knows its correct imperceptible beginning, while I am obliged to pick and choose between random sentences that say nothing to me because I'm unable to see where in the story they belong?

Therefore, I might as well use my original false beginning, which is as good as any other. There once was a cat named Mirage and so on, whatever I can come up with now. She was a calm, slightly solemn cat, just like her mother, who'd spend countless hours in the window across from the café by the post office, and who, in an earlier life, had read signs from the livers of different animals, birds, and yes, even humans.

Mirage was black with a reddish-brown tinge, and eyes of different colors. One was a radiant blue and seemed blind, the other was dark, only visible as a glimmer in the fur. Still, she was a concentrated cat. When you came in to feed her, for example, she was already poised on the kitchen chair as if she were about to eat with a fork and knife. What was strange was that she never ate anything other than liver.

That's how it went, all because she'd learned from her mother—whose name by the way I can no longer remember—that it was bad luck not to eat liver, otherwise you'd get swept away on the same day by a torrent and all its sludge and vegetable scraps from the market, and we should not think that in the end we'd fare any better than a leek top or a rotten lemon on our way down to the realm of the dead.

Ever since Mirage ran away from home, she's lived in Badinot's apartment, leaving only once when she needed to find out for herself what was going on in the street. Like the day Badinot went to jail, etc., and just about everything turned upside down.

That was last summer when you couldn't get more

than a few feet from home before it would start to rain, and Mirage wasn't farther than the café by the mailbox when it started to pour again and the square suddenly looked like the bottom of a well filling up. All around, in alcoves along the slimy walls, were small flocks of people pressed together waiting for the water to rise.

Without realizing it, Mirage was near the house where she was born, and it was here that she caught up with the lady named Natalja Valadon, who, that same morning had dared to serve her a sardine, and who just now took off her blue sandals to run across the square in bare feet.

Out in the rain, the acacia trees' supple branches were moving like flowing seaweed, and the birds had already learned to swim and they now swept by in large shoals over Mirage's head who was standing at the bottom of the deluge. Such things happen when you don't get your serving of liver and are instead let down by a sardine, in tomato sauce no less, even if you haven't so much as sniffed it.

All in all, it had turned into an utterly tragic day.

Before evening, Badinot was thrown in jail. Badinot, who always wears a cap and always uses a brown schoolbag even though he's an adult. How would he know he is Badinot when the cap and bag are taken from him and stored in a prison locker until he's released one day?

And before evening, this Natalja Valadon had moved in, bringing along two poor souls, whom she claimed were Badinot's closest friends, a little stick-legged dog of the black-white variety named Cachou, and the dog's North African boy owner, named Amman, who was compelled to scratch up with his simple knife any surface he came near. Including here in Badinot's apartment.

Mirage had a lot to deal with, strutting around and keeping order. So far, she was able to push the knife into a crack under a panel so Amman couldn't find it. Mirage also made a twenty-four-hour surveillance schedule, with roughly three-hour gaps between rounds, where she would go through the living room and kitchen, inspecting every little inch of the two hundred square feet. This is how she kept an eye on all of Badinot's fine small things, taking note of them every single day. Who knows, maybe it's just a part of a cat's superior nature to meet accidents in advance, to anticipate them, warn about them, in general, to foster awareness around the next accidental second.

This is what she's thinking as she makes her rounds, from the dresser top over to the cracked mantelpiece and iron bed and farther on to the precarious arrangements on all the kitchen shelves, from which she at last floats down to the kitchen chair across from the motionless Natalja Valadon, who, evening after evening, sits there clutching the kitchen table, longing for Badinot, whom she barely knows, knows only as you know your neighbor, but, little by little, she begins to think of him as her husband simply because she's taking care of his apartment, living there, while he's in jail temporarily doing without his beloved Mirage.

It's a disaster, and even though Mirage uses all her time inspecting, foreseeing, and calculating, something unforeseeable always happens, making everything even worse, but nevertheless, she copes with such assuredness that gradually, as a certain routine emerges, she manages to smile at Natalja Valadon, which turns out to be surprisingly unremarkable for the special language of cats.

That's how it goes, according to the present circumstances, onward, until the day when the worst, most unforeseen thing happens, the day the inheritance arrives, and Mirage has to change her thinking, yes, her whole way of thinking, her whole being.

Not because it arrived—of course it was expected now that the father, a certain Eugène Valadon, is reportedly dead—that's not what's wrong, but that it turns out to be several hundred shoeboxes, all of them presumably filled with shoes, and an entire wine cellar with endless rows of bottles, which Natalja Valadon apparently cannot store anywhere other than right here under the roof of Badinot's apartment.

From now on Mirage cannot make her rounds, cannot inspect Badinot's belongings, buried as they are under stacks of shoeboxes and wine bottles, cannot get the kind of overview from moving around in many directions and on different levels during the course of a day, and then in the evening, letting the gaze collect itself.

Now Mirage has to wait until the wine is drunk and the shoes are worn. A waiting period that might be shortened, as every morning Amman and Cachou go around the neighborhood selling both the wine and shoes, one bottle of wine or one pair of shoes per day, so there's always money for necessities, for the daily liver, of course, and a new knife for Amman.

Amman and Cachou have started to make a habit of roaming around. They aren't exactly thriving among the shoeboxes. Amman complains in particular about only being able to see above the stacked boxes in front of the window, which, in contrast, delights Mirage, who follows the day's clouds, the night's stars, and the hospital's helicopters as they travel across the sky.

This is how Mirage waits, while spending her evenings at the kitchen table with Natalja Valadon. They sit across from one another eating liver and drinking wine, and as the evening progresses and the wine takes effect, Mirage devotes herself to her newly acquired skill, a kind of movement in the body without the body itself moving, tracing in her mind, so to speak, the route her body is blocked from, following it along the walls around all the particular things in Badinot's apartment.

Apparently, it's important that I begin at the same place each evening, thinks Mirage.

Therefore, each evening, I will begin at the colored picture over the dresser of a large wooden house with a veranda painted blue and a garden leading straight down to the river to the small pier with that white pavilion. The property is only open to the side facing the river; the other three sides are surrounded by a high garden wall, and all you can see are the tops of the fruit trees in the orchard. How often I've dreamed about being a cat of that very property, going down in the evenings to the village where above the trees you can see the house's fruity towers, which at sunset must look completely golden and edible.

And on the dresser right under the picture is that Chinese crock, one of those ordinary kinds with a lid, so useful in the household, a blue dragon twisting like a rootless tree on one side. It's sitting on a little tablecloth of silk, which only seems black because as it fades over time, it reveals a pattern of pressed wet leaves, as you see in autumn on most garden paths before you think you smell snow.

And in the corner to the left of the dresser, the old travel bag belonging to, by all accounts, Napoleon's deputy, which evidently had been on the Russian campaign.

And on the mantelpiece the icon, or more correct, the mirror. One of those icons of chiseled gold or silver, where the metal forms the Madonna's dress, hair, and halo, forming a brilliant frame around an oval opening meant for her face painted on wood or canvas, which is sometimes replaced. Here the picture is missing and Badinot has replaced it with a smoky mirror, in which even a cat looks like the holy Madonna. A small photo of Viktor Blanke taken in the 1930s is stuck in the lower corner of the mirror. A young man posing near a car. His head is bare and he has a piercing gaze; his mouth is drawn in a slightly self-absorbed smile that seems almost seductive.

In the evening, when I'm done with what I've started to call my mental tour of Badinot's apartment, I hear Natalja Valadon begin to purr as she stares at the small chunks of liver I've left. She's a calm, slightly solemn cat; in one of her past lives she must have been a priest who made predictions from the livers of different animals, birds, and yes, even people. In this way, she's like my mother, whose name, by the way, I can no longer remember, but who is said to be still living down near the square in the house across from the café near the post office.

Natalja's story
about keeping your mouth shut

In the beginning we roamed the streets and never froze. The problems didn't start until Badinot got steady work and took to wearing a cap. In addition to the cap, what got him work was the little brown schoolbag he found one morning on the playground, which he always used even though he was an adult. With the help of these props, he became a courier, managing his daily route through the neighborhood himself. He took the job so seriously, he absolutely had to be alone, meaning we could no longer wander around the city together as we'd always done since we had no place to live.

It was fall, and I had spent nearly a month at a table in the café near the mailbox before Badinot provided us with a roof over our heads, a tiny room with a kitchen, plus one room on the other side of the long attic hallway, all of it high up in the sky where we were so unaccustomed to living. And because Badinot was now making money, he made all the decisions about our life, and so I was given the room, while he moved into what we called the apartment with Mirage, a very concentrated cat who'd been following us since she was tiny.

Badinot thought that this arrangement would allow us to continue to live together while seeming to live on our own so that the other residents in the building would see us as random neighbors who hardly knew each other. But soon it was revealed that everyone I met on the stairs or in the neighborhood simply called me Madame Badinot, and when I didn't correct them, Badinot finally had to give in and allow me to move freely between the room and apartment. Consequently, our life took on a certain similarity with those of the other people, and I enjoyed it every evening when I made a hot meal for Badinot and set the table with the two plates he'd procured along with the bowl and serving dish. Even though each one had a different pattern, it gave me a sense of security to touch and wash them, which I'd never known before since I grew up on the streets. This made it less important that Badinot didn't want a refrigerator or TV; it still felt like our life was becoming almost normal, although, of course, I still walked around with my plastic bag collecting things people threw away.

At this point, I was the way I'd always been, neither alone nor afraid, without any urge to find out
where I came from and what would become of me. I
never thought about why my mother left me; I simply
noted that's the way it was, that I escaped from that
orphanage—where, by the way, I had been doing so
well—and that the police had never found me. That's
why I never ended up going to school, but I learned to
read and write from my friend Jean, who was kicked
out of his house because they didn't have enough food
for him. And now, when the outside world took me
for Madame Badinot, I felt safe and didn't expect that
anyone, including myself, would need to find out who
I was. I was just here.

But I soon realized, I wouldn't get off so easily. I
never imagined I'd end up loving Badinot so much
that I'd do anything he wanted, that I'd lose myself
and become a completely different person in order
not to lose him. But that's what happened.

Badinot never told me much about his job as a
courier, just enough for me to think of it as a regular delivery service, for instance that the schoolbag,
which I rubbed with wax each week, was used to
transport all the business letters that people didn't
have the time or desire to let the post office handle.
He never let on that there were occasionally shady

deliveries. He worked every day with a strict punctuality, seeming not to give much thought to things and he could therefore easily perform his duty. That's how he gained people's trust; they'd confide in him all their thoughts and plans without realizing that he confided in no one.

One day that whole construct collapsed and he was forced to confide in me. He suddenly needed my help if he was going to succeed in becoming rich and independent once and for all. And he knew I would do anything to be drawn into his world. Indeed. I was just waiting.

It was a Tuesday, a little after noon, I was sponge bathing at the kitchen sink when he came home suddenly and threw the schoolbag on the table.

—Do you think you can keep your mouth shut if you have to? he asked, pouring two glasses of wine as if we were going to seal a pact.

—Yes, I said, drying off and reaching for my clothes.

—No, you need to put on something else. He pulled out a silk dress with a dense flower pattern from his bag and then a dark-blue cardigan and tossed them at me. I put them on and danced around excitedly. Badinot stopped me and placed a pair of blue sandals before my feet. I put them on and we stood there with raised glasses, and I felt as if I were finally married to Badinot, just as I'd always wanted.

—You promise to do what I tell you? he asked. —Otherwise it won't work.

—Yes, I said, putting down the glass. —Yes, if I can.

We sat down at the table across from each other.

—You know, one can do whatever one wants, I added kindly.

—No, answered Badinot. —One can do what one must.

Then he pulled out a dark-blue shoulder bag, such a one as I've always wanted, but instead of handing it to me, he opened it and emptied out the contents. Handkerchief, makeup and lipstick. Passport and papers. Pen and notebook. Checkbook, wallet, and keys. Comb and perfume. A chestnut and an old movie ticket.

—I didn't realize you stole it, I said, disappointed. —I thought you found something no one needed.

—It's that, too, Badinot said. —The woman it belonged to was found dead a couple of hours ago. By me.

I shivered under the silk dress and pulled the blue cardigan up over my shoulders.

—You can say I've stolen it. But I've stolen it from a corpse that will never again have any need for it, said Badinot, placing a diamond ring, a watch, and a string of pearls on the table between us.

I put them on immediately and began my life as Natalja Valadon.

Badinot fished two shiny hair clips out of his pocket, and I put my hair up just like the photo in her passport. I studied the passport and papers, imprinting myself with my birthdate and address, and then I put everything carefully back into the bag, all according to Badinot's orders, who, meanwhile, went over what had happened and what I would have to do. There was no time to waste.

It turned out that Badinot had gone, as usual, to Valadon's factory to pick up a delivery. When he got there, no one was around, but it had happened before that the workers had been sent home due to a material shortage. So, he went to see if anyone was in the office. No one answered when he rang the bell. He tried the door; it wasn't locked so he went in. Not a sound to be heard, but at the end of the hall, the door to Valadon's office was wide open. Badinot didn't expect to find anyone, but went down there anyway. It wasn't until he was inside the room that he saw the bodies. Valadon, his wife, and daughter. Whether a stranger had murdered them or Valadon himself had taken his family with him to his death was not clear. The entire scene seemed so unreal that in the first few moments, Badinot forgot that he should notify the police, and when he thought of it later, he did not because in the meantime he'd become so obsessed with an idea that it was impossible to shake it off.

He stood there—he didn't know how long —as if paralyzed, staring down at the daughter who lay stretched out on the floor, completely convinced that it was me. The resemblance was that striking. It wasn't until the tears welled up in his eyes and he saw her expensive jewelry glinting that he realized his mistake. But by then the fateful idea that I should take over her life now that she could no longer live it had already taken hold of him.

That's what happened. He took her belongings and disposed of her body, never telling me how. Then, as said, he handed over her clothes and everything else and sent me "home to myself," as he said, with instructions for how I should act if this or that happened.

Still, I had no idea what to do. And when I turned the key in the door and entered her apartment, I started shaking all over thinking that maybe there were others who had keys, maybe I was married and my husband would soon come home, or maybe I had a friend who'd show up later that evening. I forced myself not to think about it and started to examine the apartment systematically to find out as much as possible about myself.

It wasn't until late in the evening, when the police rang the doorbell and told me that my parents were found dead, that I completely broke down and cried so hard, I didn't think I'd ever stop.

But as the days pass, I've in fact become used to my life as Valadon, who, it turns out, has clothes for every occasion and apparently no regular employment. No one makes any demands on her, no man, no friends or family. Only a couple of my father's business relations called to express their condolences, without asking anything from me.

Pale but composed, I attended my parents' funeral and met with the different lawyers managing the estate. That's how I got to know the extent of my wealth. I didn't have to worry about giving Badinot money for new clothes so we could look acceptable going out to eat together. In this way, he could pursue his plans for our future, which seemed finally to include us getting married in Natalja Valadon's church.

In the meantime, I had a lot of stress from my exhaustive research trying to figure out who I really was. Not every day. I believe I behaved more or less in conformity with my person. Except in relation to the sale of my father's shoe factory; it was probably a big mistake that I demanded more than a thousand shoeboxes all containing the same shoe in my size to be removed from the business. The outrage wasn't so much over the quantity as the style, which seemed folksy, not for Eugène Valadon's customers, but for his daughter at least.

No, what really caused me stress was my attempt to

penetrate my own and my family's past. There weren't many photos. And the written things I found cleaning up after my mother and father were almost all letters that were postmarked in Copenhagen and apparently written in Danish. The same goes for a little poem, which I found crumpled up in between my mother's jewelry, and which I always carry with me in my purse because I later took a Danish course and can now easily read it, although it still seems somewhat alien. It contains no family secrets and so I'm not revealing anything by reading it.

> *If you think I have blue-black hair*
> *think again, I've dyed it flaxen fair,*
> *well, maybe its color is blonde.*
>
> *I have showy summer breasts,*
> *but since winter's shivering body never rests*
> *they'll turn small in your freezing hand.*
>
> *My soul takes its color from the air's tint,*
> *my beauty comes and away it creeps,*
> *it's best when I'm known for the scent*
> *of wild strawberries, onions, and sheep.*
>
> *It's best if nothing happens.*
> *It's best if we never meet.*
>
> *But it's even better if something's born*
> *from all the visions we see,*
> *a blind longing for more.*

I found many more things in my own drawers. Not so many letters, but volumes of notes and sketches for longer prose works, in fact an entire draft of a short story, and detailed rejection letters from different publishers. It was extremely difficult for me to know which were my real experiences and which were manifestations of Natalja Valadon's urge to express herself.

For example, there's a description of a house that's returned to again and again, a large wooden house with a veranda that was painted blue, and a garden leading straight down to the river with a small pier and a white pavilion. Several times it's noted how the property was only opened to the side facing the river; the three other sides were surrounded by a high garden wall and all you could see were the tops of the fruit trees in the orchard. But down in the village you could see the house's fruity towers, which at sunset looked golden and edible.

This description reminded me a lot of the scene on the colored brochure that Badinot had hanging for a year over the dresser in our little apartment; he'd found it a year ago in a shopping cart over in the supermarket.

As time passed and I immersed myself more and more in these writings, everything became clear to me—I had to write it all out again in a more logical way if my family's history was ever going to make sense to me.

And so last summer, when you couldn't get more than a few feet from home before it would start to rain, I'd one day made it all the way down to the café near the mailbox and it started to pour again. The square looked like the bottom of a well filling up. All around in alcoves along the slimy walls were small flocks of people pressed together waiting for the water to rise. Finally, I got tired of waiting. I took off my blue sandals and put them in the plastic bag and pressed them against my chest. Then, in bare feet, I ran across the street. The water came up to my ankles, and the raindrops bounced so high from the asphalt that they splashed under my dress. My dress got soaked in the short time it took me to reach the café and was clinging to my body. Inside the café, a thick steam hung in the air from all the wet clothes, and the voices sounded like a tropical hum. I squeezed myself down at a table facing the street and there I sat. I'd never set out to write anything before. I think it had something to do with the tightly packed room, the atmosphere of thick steam coming off all the creatures washed ashore into this café, now chatting and laughing so that their voices remained in the air. It was as calming as the rain's violent sound, drowning out my sentences, making me unafraid to write them.

For many months I continued to write, sometimes at home, sometimes at the café, all over, and I was transformed. Even when I was with Badinot, I told him all that my family had experienced without pause, and after a while he feared for my sanity if we didn't get married immediately.

Therefore, the date was set, but as soon as the wedding was announced, I received the following letter: Natalja Valadon cannot get married because Natalja Valadon is dead. Signed, Viktor Blanke.

Immediately, I was gripped by panic, for I had left out that exact figure Viktor Blanke from my rewriting of the family history because I was certain he was pure fiction.

Now that he exists, it's possible that he could be Natalja Valadon's murderer. And if he could murder her once, he could also murder her twice.

Or, he knew who the murderer was. Maybe he also knew that Badinot had removed the body. Or knew that Badinot was the murderer? No.

As if in a trance, I left my apartment and went over to Badinot's. He wasn't home yet, so I let myself in. When I walked in, Mirage was already poised on the kitchen chair as if she were about to eat with a fork and knife. She's a calm, slightly solemn cat, and her eyes are different colors. One is a radiant blue and seems blind, the other is dark and appears as a glimmer in the fur. Anyway, she's a very concentrated cat. There was no food to be found anywhere, however, so I gave her nothing, and hurried to pack my bag with my old clothes and other belongings, finally placing the Chinese crock and the colored brochure with the wooden house and the blue-painted veranda in the middle of my bag to protect them. Then I kissed Mirage and took off.

How I ended up in Copenhagen, steering right into that disaster, is a longer story. But if only I had kept my mouth shut from the beginning, it never would have happened.

I never should have committed to memory that story my grandmother predicted about me. If I hadn't been able to remember what was going to happen, what was now happening wouldn't have been able to occur. When she wasn't even my grandmother. And maybe not even Natalja Valadon's grandmother.

I never should have told Badinot about how she pointed at the Chinese crock, turning it a little so I could see the blue dragon twisting like a rootless tree on one side of it, since Badinot now had a crock that perfectly matched those ordinary ones with lids, so useful in the household, in which for a long time he'd kept all the buttons we'd find on our forays through the city.

In any case, I should not have said she made me promise, when it was time, to put my mother's ashes in that crock and bring it back to Denmark so she could be buried in the same place she was born. In any case, I wouldn't have known that this promise would live inside me as a kind of compulsion, meaning that sooner or later I would have to carry out the order regardless if I had the wrong contents—neither my mother's ashes, since I've never known my mother, nor Natalja Valadon's mother's ashes, which were taken care of long ago in the usual way after I finally read and understood what should be done with them. There was no urn at all. Just an ordinary crock, full of buttons, perhaps. But if someone asks me, I'd rather have them believe it's filled with pickled ginger, or maybe blackberries with sugar and vodka, or sour cream, cheese, lard, or spices perhaps. Or simply tea. Badinot always finds so many things on his route as a courier.

Natalja's story about nothing

It was late in the summer. I went for a walk in the cemetery, not to visit a particular grave, but just to get some relief from my city life. I wound my way around the graves and then continued up the steep main road when I was suddenly overtaken by a powerful cloud burst. Everyone sought shelter under the trees, and there we lined up with small spaces between us, like guards on a mourning route waiting for the storm to pass. But it only came down harder, and soon the rain broke through the canopy of leaves and there was no point standing there. Those with umbrellas, newspapers, or other forms of protection walked with determination into the rain. Only a Japanese man closed his umbrella and entered one of the mausoleums where he stood next to a gray angel. I watched him indecisively, as if considering doing the same, but I was too afraid to get close to death in there, and besides, the sky had become as dark as the earth. And once everything is in one, you'll try at any cost to get out of it.

And so, with sandals in hand, I took off through the rushing water, which came up to my legs down by the lower-lying exit. I saw it falling like water stairs down over a stony mound, taking soil and torn plants in its path. I leapt across the road halfway into the flower shop where many were already seeking shelter. I grabbed the bottom of my dress and was wringing out the water when a young man bumped into me, knocking over a bucket of dahlias. He handed me the entire bunch, leaving me standing there with them in my arms as he went over to the rushing gutter to refill the bucket.

I stood there staring ahead aimlessly and then put the dahlias into the bucket. He pulled his T-shirt off and wrung it out hard.

—I saw you in the cemetery, he said. —I was running right behind you.

He shook out his T-shirt, but didn't put it on. I was freezing because I was wet, and my skin was bluish.

—I know how we can get your clothes dried, he said, taking my hand.

—It doesn't matter, I said.

—Come on, I know a bathhouse. He took off with me. —It's just two blocks from here.

I didn't even give it a thought; I just let myself be carried along, and on top of that, to a bathhouse. As if I weren't wet enough already. We just ran and I laughed as the puddles splashed around us. I didn't care that my skirt was so soaked that you could almost see my skin. I could've run through the whole city if I had to, that's how trusting I felt.

And before I knew it, I was sitting in one of the bathhouse's deep tubs, enjoying the warm water and the sharp smell of soap.

The young man—I didn't even know his name— had insisted that I leave my dress and underwear with the bath attendant, who would bring them to the counter where he was waiting because he intended to run to the nearest laundromat to get them dried.

What if he doesn't come back, I thought. Then I'll have to borrow one of the bathhouse's white robes and wander home in it; I'll seem like an insane person escaping from the hospital. But how else would I get home? I knew no one, no one who loved me, and therefore there was no one who'd come help without mocking me and demanding an explanation. Not one single person. I might as well not exist. I meant nothing.

I smiled when I realized that this situation was actually what I'd been waiting for. I slid deeper into the water and rejoiced over the relief of my thoughts. Basically, it was just fine that I didn't mean anything to anyone; this way, I could easily slip out of my life without anyone noticing.

I emerged splashing out of the tub as if reborn. The bath attendant called out from the other room, asking if she could scrub my back. I said, no thank you, I didn't need her help until I got my clothes back. Suddenly, it was clear to me what was going to happen. I took my bag and emptied its contents onto the stool. I ripped up all the cards and papers with my name on them into small pieces.

I cut the plastic cards in strips with my fruit knife. Then I flushed everything down the toilet. I had to flush four times before everything went down, letting the water drain from the bathtub the whole time to not be too conspicuous.

I sat on the edge of the bathtub watching my image disappear in the last rushing vortex around the toilet bowl. I've always dreamed about being someone else, traveling to a foreign city and beginning again. And now I sat there naked, with only a cigarette, while I slowly but surely transformed. Soon there'd only be one insignificant remainder of Natalja Valadon. I smoothed my hair back and gathered it in an elastic band at my neck. Who should I become? What should I call myself? Jeanne maybe. I could just as well choose the first and best name that occurred to me. My lips have the same color as red peppers. Jeanne de Piment. I was parentless and had spent my childhood and youth on the streets. So far, nothing more was needed to know about myself.

When the dress arrived, I put it on and left the steamy room. Well, he was standing there waiting for me. He had on his T-shirt. It had apparently been dried along with the dress. I touched it as I said thank you. He also had on a little cap that I hadn't noticed before, and in his hand, a schoolbag. As if there were a purpose to his existence.

That's how it went, that's how I first met Badinot, as he called himself, and since that day we've been inseparable. Naturally, I introduced myself as Jeanne de Piment. He smiled as if he approved of the name, and when I told him that I was homeless, I sensed immediately that he'd never leave my side. He didn't say anything particular about himself, only that we couldn't really go to his place, but he knew of somewhere else we could stay, at least for a few nights, and it was enough to make me happy about my new life.

There we lay stretched out next to each other on some sacks in a warehouse down by the freight-rail yard with a couple of empty sack cloths pulled over us. He kissed me on the forehead before we went to sleep and when we woke up.

It was now decided that Badinot would look for a place for us, somewhere to live, and he'd do it alone, because he always worked alone when it was really important, and so meanwhile I had to pass the time, and he knew of a café where you could spend the whole day without ordering much if you couldn't afford it, and so there I was placed at his usual table with a cup of coffee, a pack of cigarettes, and some lined stationery, which I quietly and calmly set out to fill so that I could at any time delineate my world from those around me.

This is how I wrote a great deal of what my grandmother had told me, or, more correctly, what Natalja Valadon's grandmother had told her, which I could easily pretend that I myself had made up now that in the future I will never be called anything other than Jeanne de Piment.

I also managed to write a longer story about a young woman who stole Natalja Valadon's identity. It happened in such a way that a man, based on Badinot, finds Natalja and her parents murdered and is struck by Natalja's likeness to the young woman he loves, who, for that matter, I might as well have called Jeanne de Piment, but in the story is nameless. That man I call Badinot deposes of Natalja's body and takes her elegant clothes and belongings home so the young woman can disguise herself and pose as the heir of the Valadon family. Later, the plan was to burn Natalja's body somewhere near the freight-rail yard so that the ashes could be collected in an urn and given the name of the young woman, which might as well be Jeanne de Piment. And her urn might just be the one right beside me now. In that case, the ashes in there would be a copy of myself.

But in the real world, everything went in another direction.

Badinot and I hadn't lived together for long before the tragedy revealed itself.

Suddenly one day my own father was murdered by my mother's lover. At exactly the same time, Badinot also attempted to murder my father, but the bullet accidentally hit the lover, who usually went by the name of Viktor Blanke, and who by the way had also been my lover. And, in earlier days, my grandmother's. When my mother committed suicide at Viktor Blanke's funeral, and when Badinot refused to reveal his motives for wanting to take my father's life and was thrown in jail, he said he didn't want me to visit, and so eventually it became meaningless to think of myself as Jeanne de Piment or Natalja Valadon. There was nothing left. Nothing of what I was running from. And nothing of what I'd longed for. There were only the practical things needing to be done. And these I did as well as I now could. I cleaned up after the dead, I hired the best lawyer for Badinot, I let Amman and Cachou roam around as they wished, and I placed Mirage in the care of a cat lover, and then took off with my mother's urn so that it could be buried in Copenhagen just as my grandmother had wished.

I brought a stack of my father's and mother's personal papers and letters on the journey. And as I was sitting on the train somewhere in the mountains—which I called the Tatra Mountains although I knew very well that they were located somewhere else in the world—I found among my father's papers the information that Badinot was his son with someone other than my mother.

Suddenly, it was as if the earth had disappeared from under the train and I was thrown up in the air where it felt like I floated for an eternity before falling and striking my head on something hard. In reality—I remember this clearly—nothing had happened. I sat there as I'd been sitting the whole time. The train went along as it had the entire trip. Only, I couldn't hear it. It was completely quiet in my head. Everything had disappeared inside there. Nothing was left of all that I had heard about and experienced my entire life. Including all that I had hoped and dreamed.

I couldn't even dream about starting over. Anyway, I smiled when I realized that this was the situation I had waited for. At last I did not have a choice. I was simply forced to continue. Just continue. As a second Natalja Valadon.